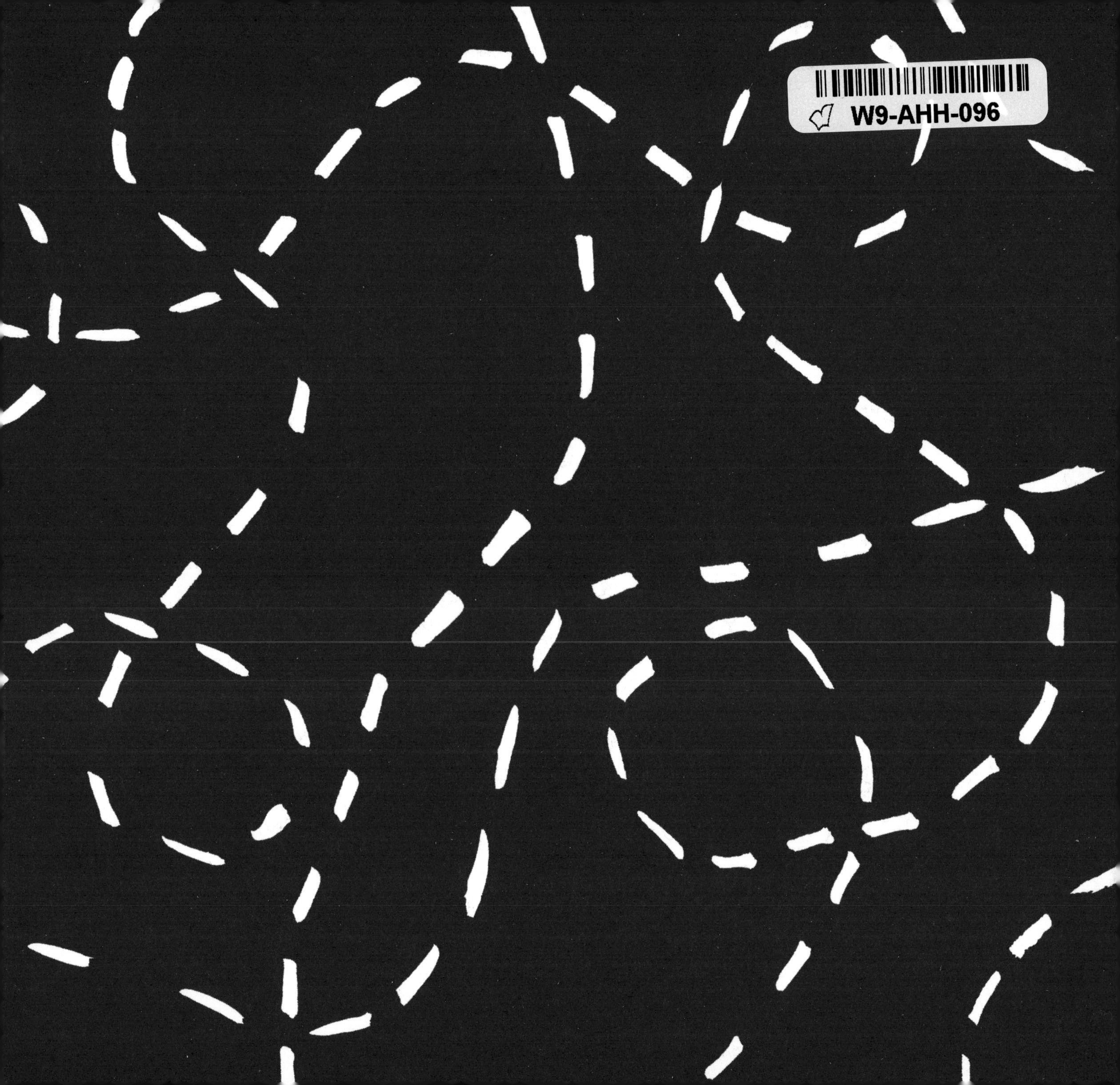

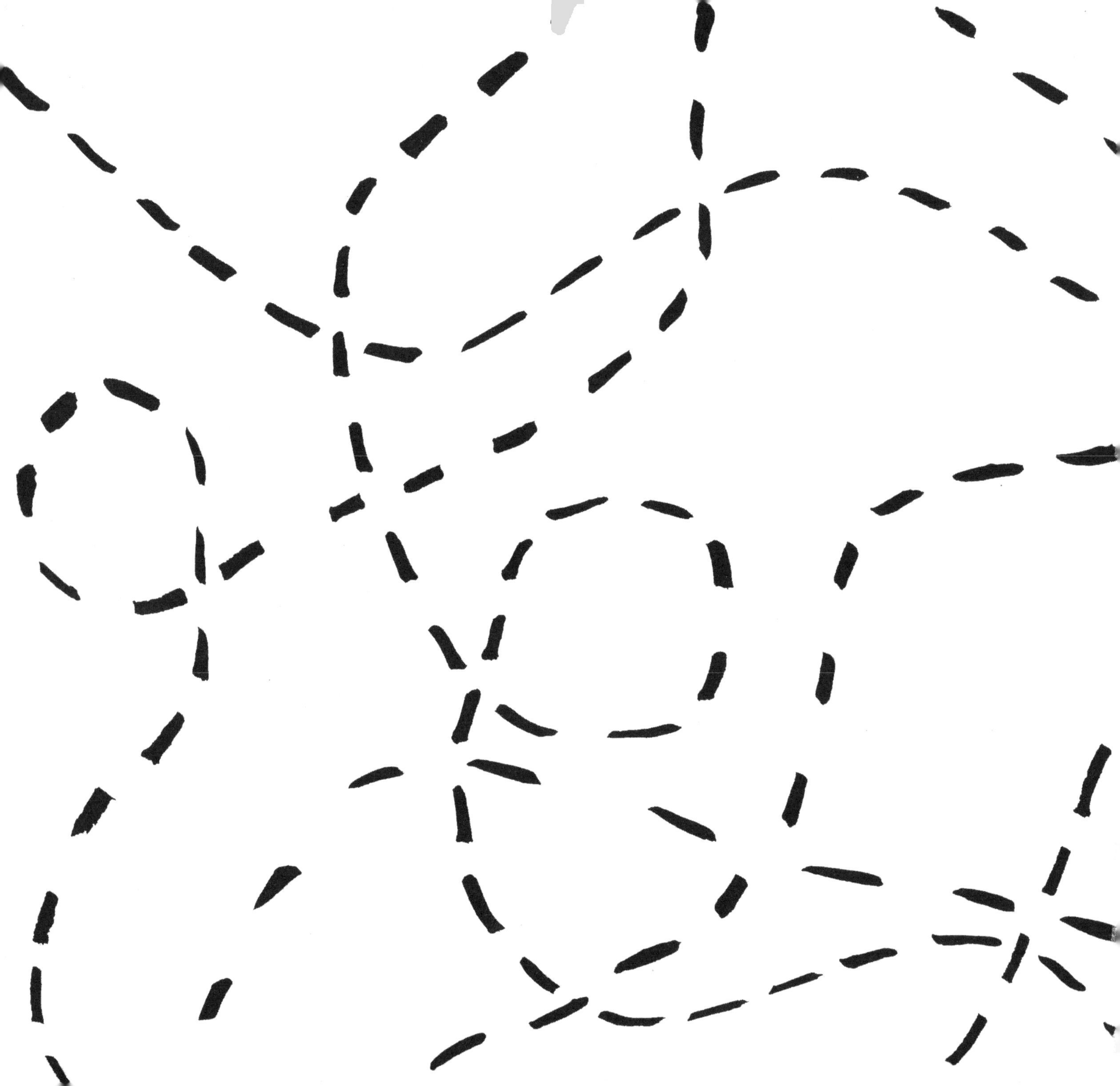

Written by Ziggy Hanaor
Illustrated by Alice Bowsher

It was a beautiful, sunny day in the park,
and Fly was having fun practising her flying.

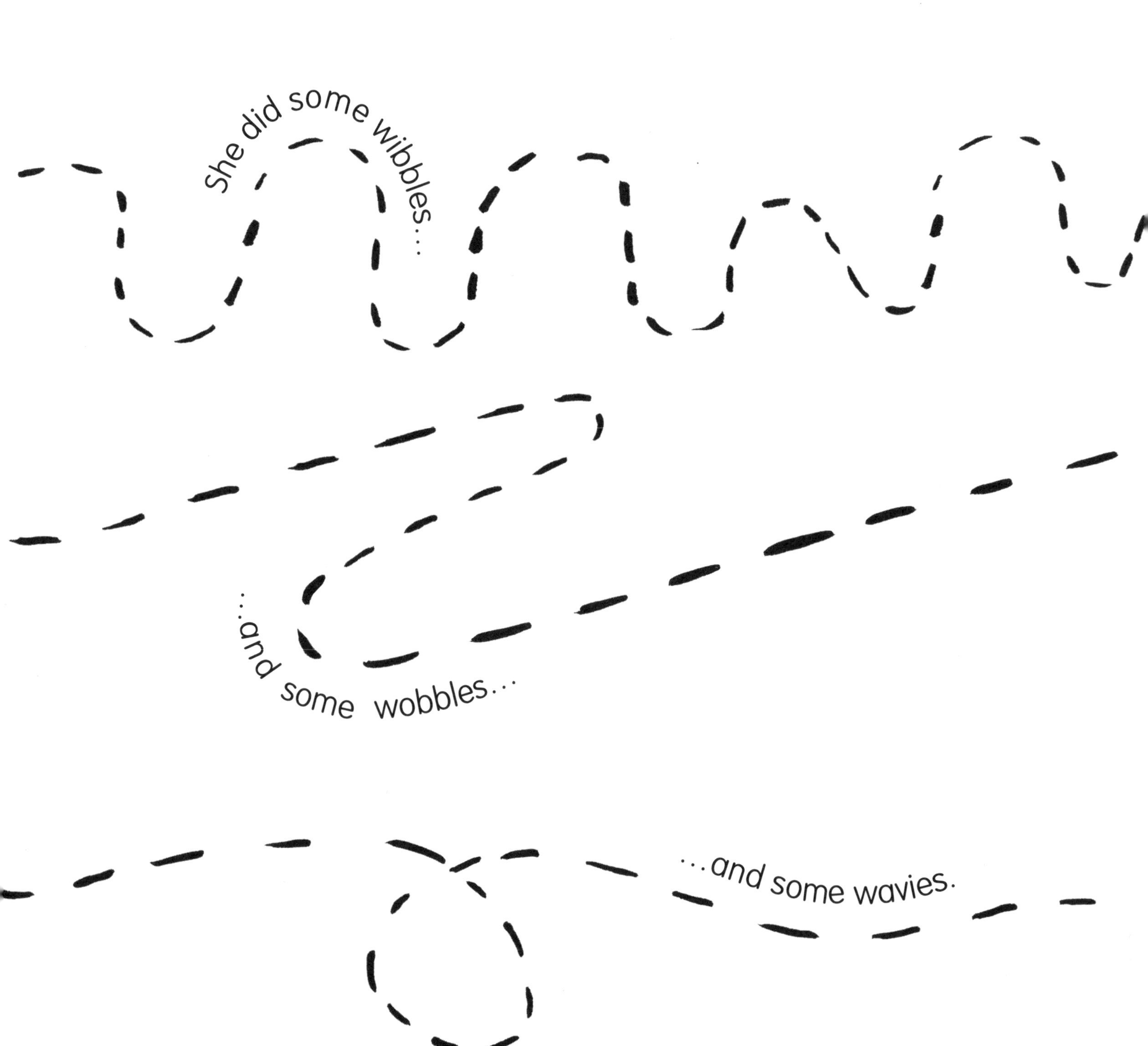
She did some wibbles…
…and some wobbles…
…and some wavies.

'What are you doing?' asked Blackbird.

'I'm flying,' replied Fly.

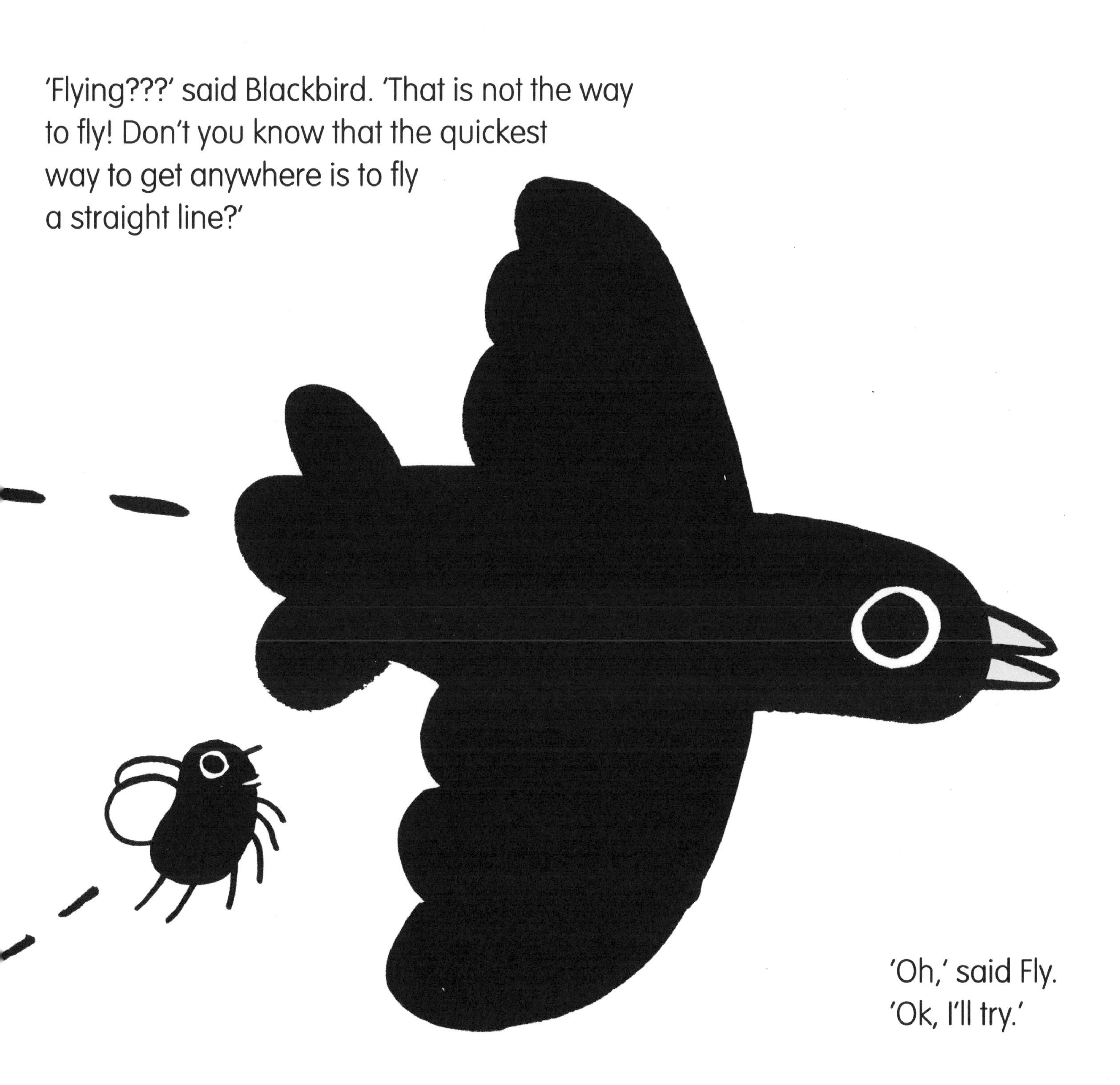

'Flying???' said Blackbird. 'That is not the way to fly! Don't you know that the quickest way to get anywhere is to fly a straight line?'

'Oh,' said Fly.
'Ok, I'll try.'

Fly concentrated very hard on flying in a straight line,
but try as she might, she couldn't help wobbling all over the place.

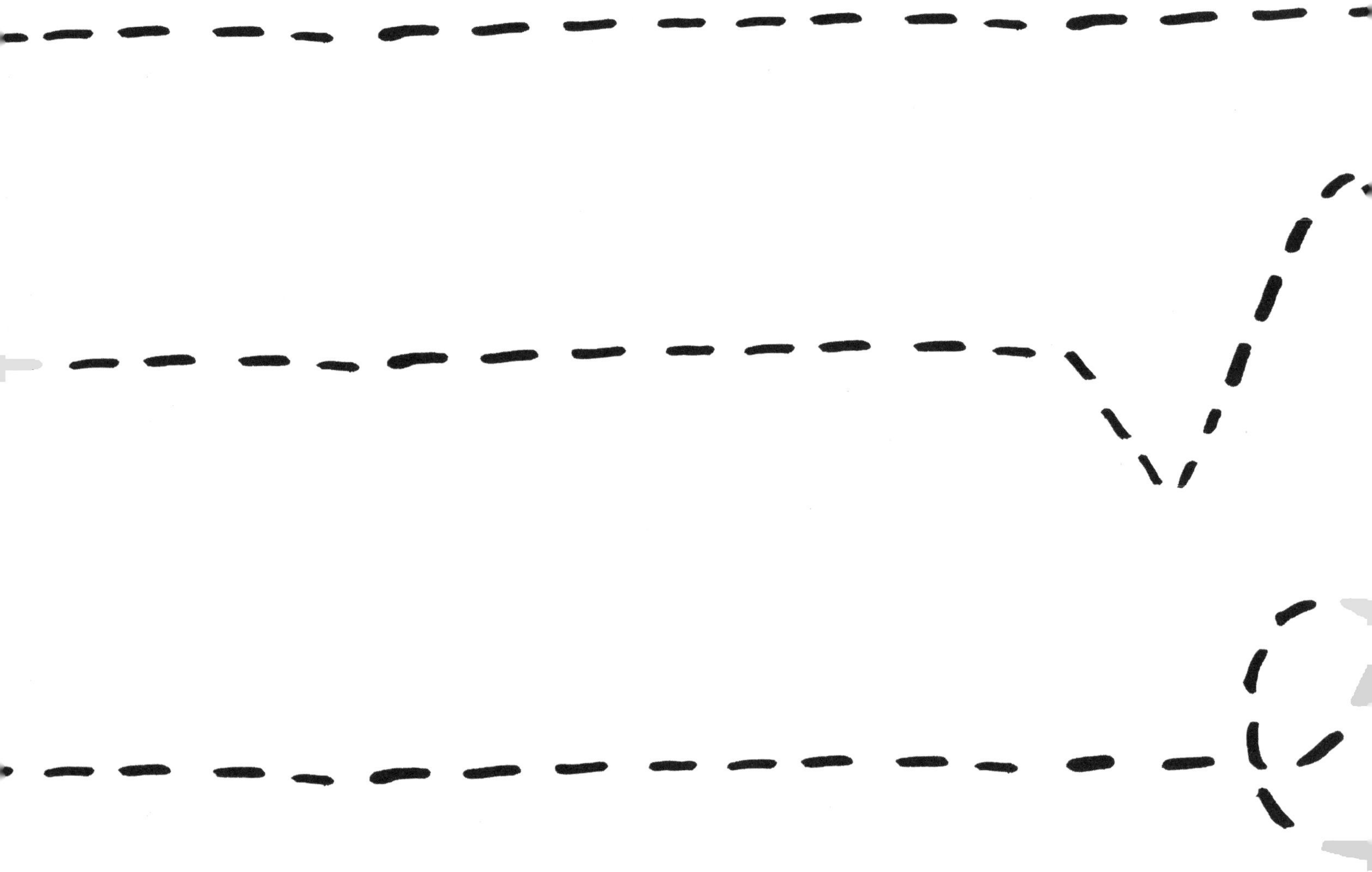

'Hmph,' said Fly.
'That is not my way to fly.'

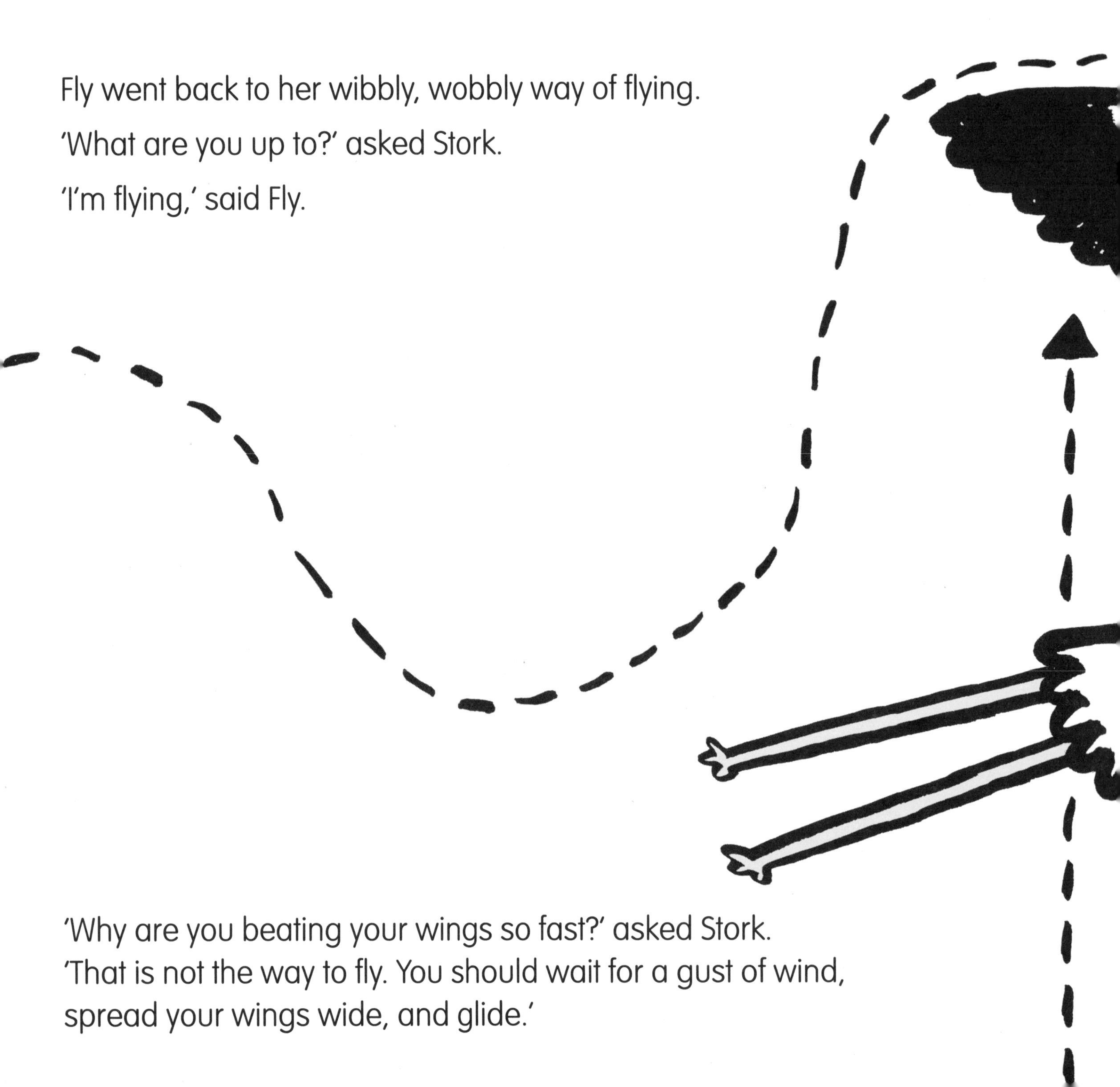

Fly went back to her wibbly, wobbly way of flying.

'What are you up to?' asked Stork.

'I'm flying,' said Fly.

'Why are you beating your wings so fast?' asked Stork.
'That is not the way to fly. You should wait for a gust of wind,
spread your wings wide, and glide.'

'Alright,' said Fly.
'I'll give it a try.'

So Fly waited for a big gust of wind and stretched out her wings as far as they would go.

The wind blew her straight into a tree.

'OW!' yelled Fly.
'That is NOT my way to fly.'

Fly went back to her buzzy, flappy way of flying.

'What's up?' asked Starling.

'I'm flying, of course,' said Fly.

'All on your own?' asked Starling, horrified. 'That is not the way to fly! You need to take to the sky with all your friends, swooping and diving together like one big bird.'

'That does sound fun,' said Fly.
'I'll give it a try.'

So Fly tried to find some friends, but the other flies weren't that interested. And when they did fly together, they just got in each other's way.

'This isn't fun at all,' said Fly.
'This is not my way to fly.'

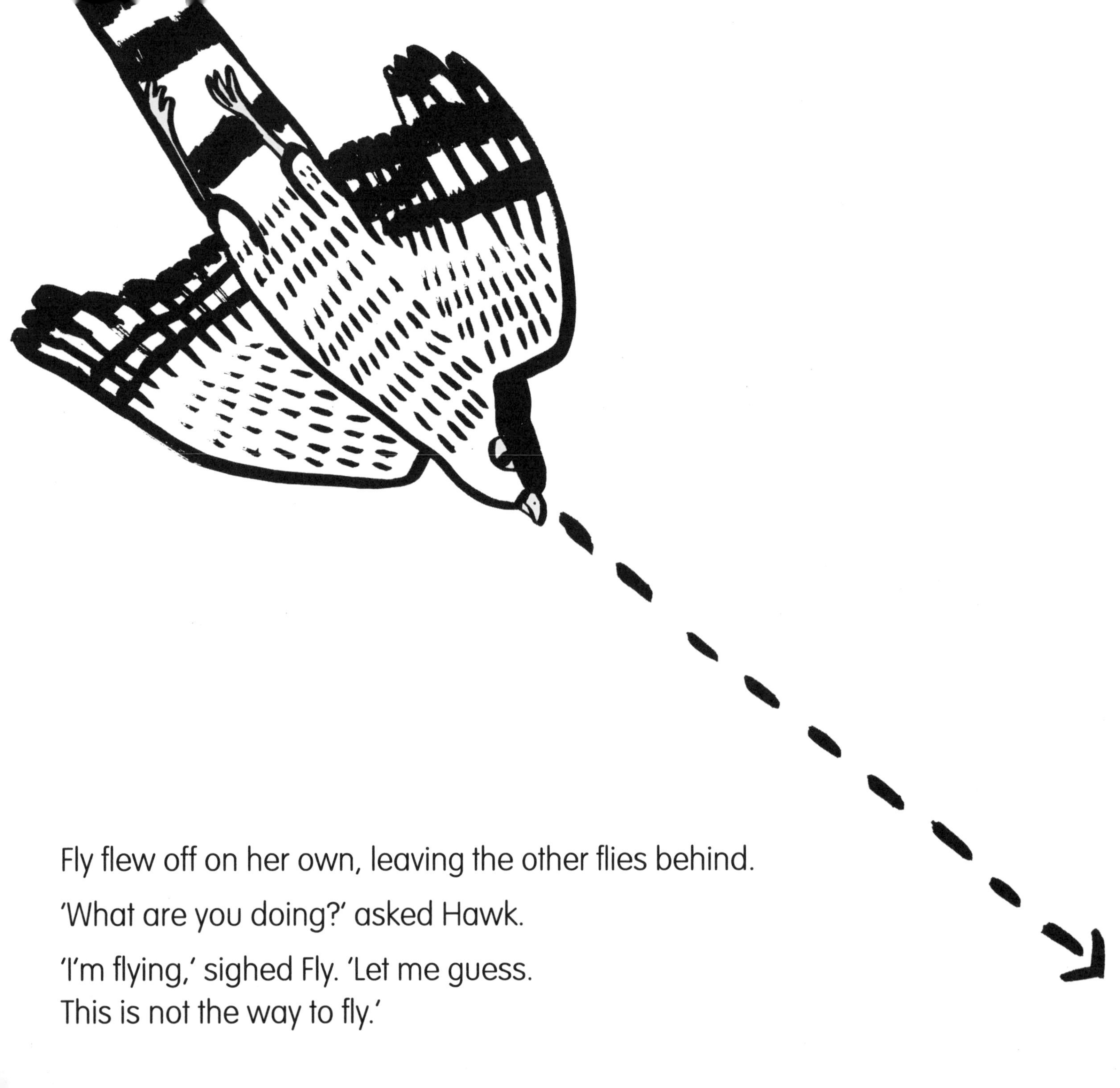

Fly flew off on her own, leaving the other flies behind.

'What are you doing?' asked Hawk.

'I'm flying,' sighed Fly. 'Let me guess.
This is not the way to fly.'

'You're right,' said Hawk. 'That is NOT the way to fly. You need to fly up high and get your food in your sights. When you're sure it can't run away, dive straight down, nab it and swoop back up again.'

Fly rolled her eyes.
'I guess I'll give it a try.'

So Fly found a tasty looking sandwich and flew up as high as she could. When she was sure the sandwich wasn't going to run away...

'Uuurgh,' groaned Fly.
'That is not my way to fly.'

So Fly went back to her way of flying.

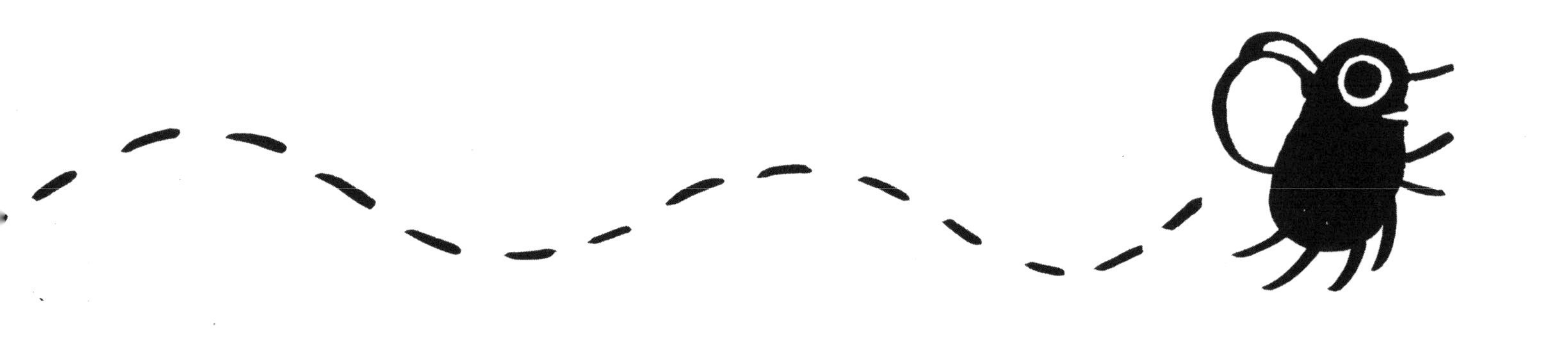

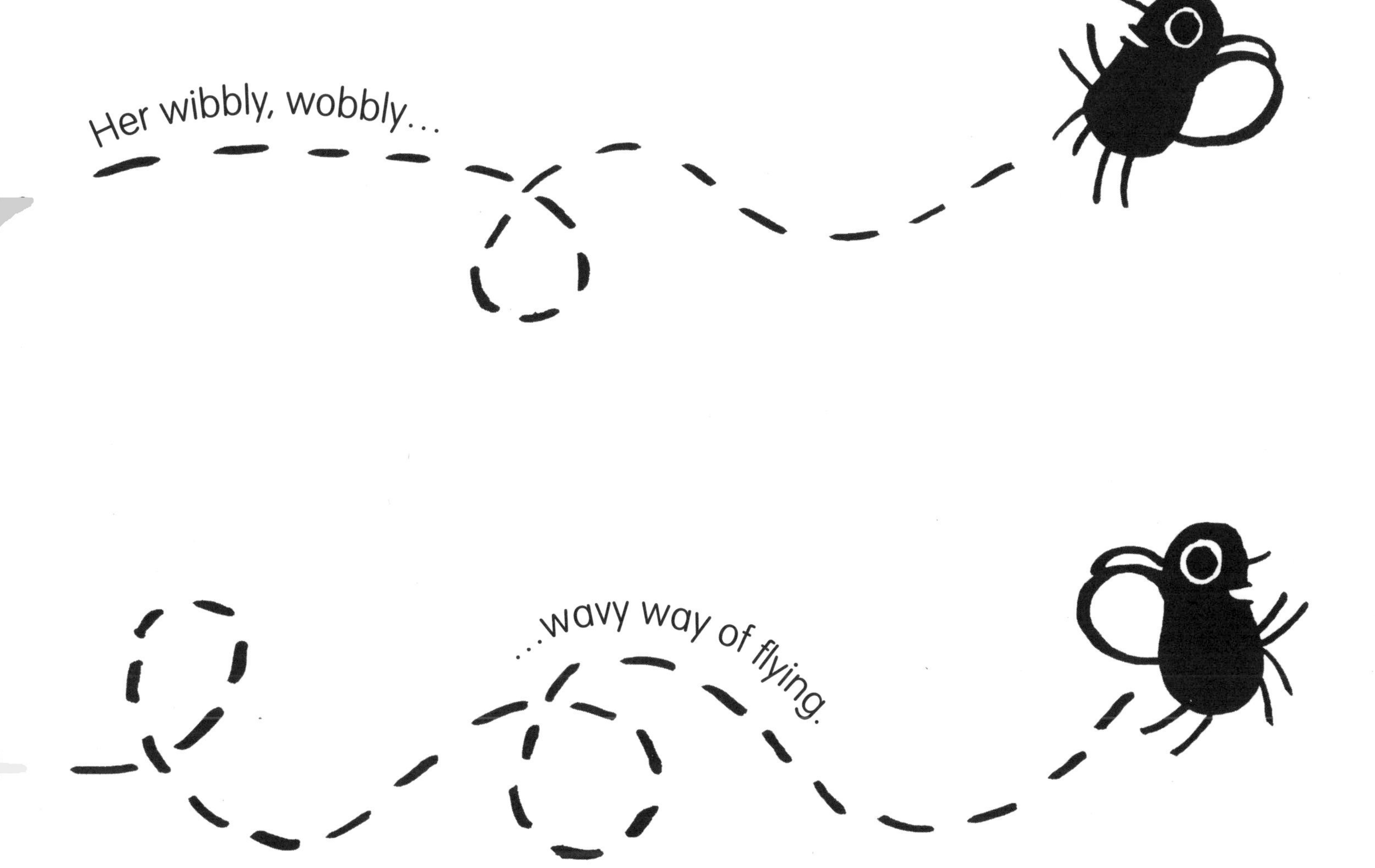

The sun was shining bright
and the grass smelled sweet.

'What are you up to?' asked Butterfly.

Fly ignored her.

'Excuse me,' said Butterfly. 'I just –'

`I DON'T WANT

SHOUTED FLY. `I DON'T
LINE, AND I DON'T WANT
AND I DON'T WANT
AND I DON'T WANT

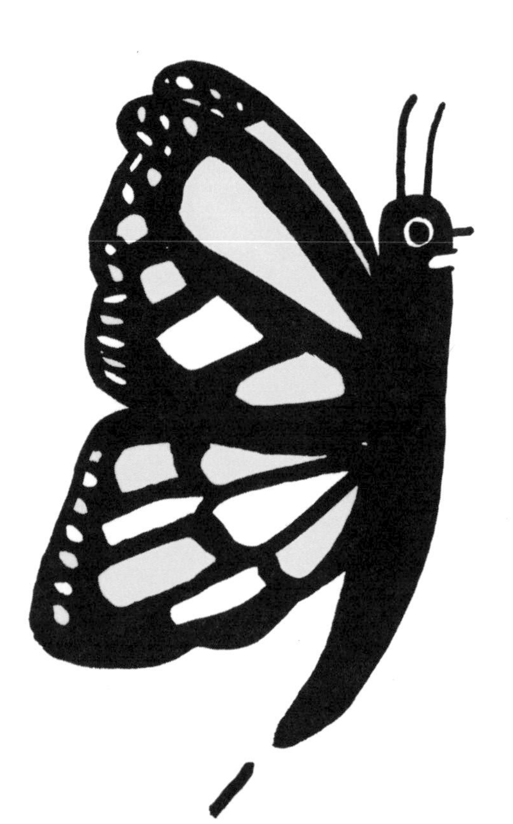

THIS IS

AND I

TO HEAR IT!'

WANT TO FLY IN A STRAIGHT
TO GLIDE ON THE WIND,
TO FLY IN A FLOCK,
TO DIVE ONTO MY FOOD.

HOW I FLY
LIKE IT!'

'I like it too,' said Butterfly.
'I wanted to say,
you've got good moves.'

'Really?' said Fly.

'Yes. I'm heading to that flower over there. Want to come?'

'Ok,' said Fly.

And off they flew.

fly flies

Written by Ziggy Hanaor
Illustrated by Alice Bowsher
Designed by Mélanie Dautreppe-Liermann

British Library Cataloguing-in-Publication Data.
A CIP record for this book is available from the British Library.

ISBN: 978-1-908714-61-9

First published in 2019 by:
Cicada Books Ltd
48 Burghley Road
London, NW5 1UE

www.cicadabooks.co.uk